Every Road Leads Back To You

By: Britt Wolfe

Cover design, formatting, and caffeine consumption by Britt Wolfe. Additional emotional support provided by Sophie and Lena.

First Edition: 2025

Printed in Canada because books deserve a solid passport stamp too.

If you enjoyed this book, please consider leaving a review. If you didn't, well, that's between you and your questionable taste.

This Novella Is Dedicated to:

Taylor Swift whose extraordinary storytelling through music has been a source of endless inspiration. Your words and melodies remind us of the beauty in love, heartbreak, and the journey of finding ourselves.

And to all the artists who pour their hearts into their craft, lighting the way for dreamers like me and so many others – you remind us that are has the power to heal, connect, and transform. Thank you for showing us the magic of creation and the courage it takes to share it with the world.

Every Road Leads Back To You
Is Inspired by: *Our Song* and *Tis The Damn Season*
by Taylor Swift

SSince Evermore graced us back in 2020, Tis the Damn Season has always felt like a continuation of Our Songto me—a glimpse of what happens when the golden simplicity of young love collides with the complexities of growing up. It's the ache of something once so effortless, now fractured by time and choices. It's the pull of home, of the person who feels like home, and the bittersweet reality of knowing you can never quite go back—yet you'll never quite let go.

This story, inspired by Taylor Swift's extraordinary words, is my ode to the beauty of love that was impossibly young, impossibly innocent, and heartbreakingly fleeting. It's about letting go, the pain of losing something that shaped you, and the endless, soul-deep search to feel it again.

I hope it resonates with you the way Taylor's songs always have with me.

Peace, Love, and Inspiration,

Britt Wolfe

The Places We Leave And The People We Can't

The icy Pennsylvania winter greeted me the moment I stepped off the bus, its sharp chill biting at my cheeks. I'd hated this cold growing up—hated how it crept into every crack and refused to let go—but now, it felt like an old, familiar embrace. My breath rose in soft, billowing clouds, carrying with it memories of a simpler time: building lopsided snowmen in the front yard, twirling under the glow of the winter carnival lights, stringing Christmas bulbs around the porch with frozen fingers, and baking in our cramped little kitchen with Mom. The evenings always ended the same—with steaming mugs of apple cider by the fire, Dad's laugh warming the room as the snow fell softly outside.

Being back now, after all this time, I felt close to all that had been. Still, those moments also felt impossibly distant now, like a snow globe I could still see but would never quite touch again.

I thought about Dad as I rubbed my hands together, trying to chase away the cold while waiting for a taxi to pull up to the curb. I hadn't told him I was coming. How could I? After everything we'd been through—time stretching like a chasm between us, pulling us into estrangement, the loss of Mom carving its own hollow in our lives, and all the quiet, unspoken hurts that had settled in the spaces where love used to fit so easily. The years had left their marks on us, lines etched into our faces, the weight of grief and distance pressing down on our shoulders. How do you tell someone you're coming back when the road between you feels so broken?

I hadn't come home for Mom's funeral. Instead, I spent that week—just as I had so many weeks before and after—in the company of my closest companion: vodka. I drank until the edges of my pain blurred, until I felt nothing at all. And while I numbed myself, Dad bore the weight of it alone, facing her loss without me. Now, after all this time, I'm finally on my way back—to his home, to the scene of so many hurts and the place I left him to grieve alone.

I climbed into the first taxi that pulled up to the bus station, sliding into the backseat as the driver turned to glance at me. His face stopped me mid-motion—he was my age and looked vaguely familiar.

"Willa Barrett?" he asked, his voice a mix of surprise and, maybe—just maybe—a hint of excitement.

I met his gaze in the rearview mirror, my blank expression betraying the gap in my memory, the years that had stolen the name and story behind his face.

"Blake Bailey," he prompted gently, and suddenly, the memories fell into place all at once, like scattered puzzle pieces clicking together. Blake Bailey, young and handsome, thrower of many debaucherous parties and close friend to my high school sweetheart.

"Of course," I said, forcing a smile—the kind I'd perfected in Hollywood, polished and practiced but never quite reaching my eyes.

"You here for the holidays?" Blake asked as he pulled away from the curb. "Heading to your parents' place?"

He was already navigating the familiar turns toward the small rectangular house I grew up in. As a kid, it had never felt like enough—too small, too ordinary for the dreams I carried back then. But now, it called to me with an irresistible pull, as though it were the only place left where I could catch my breath.

"Yes, and yes," I replied, pulling a small compact from my leather carry-on —the only luggage I'd brought with me from Los Angeles. I flipped it open and began primping in the tiny mirror, though I wasn't sure why or who I was doing it for. Maybe it was nerves, or maybe it was just that flicker of superficiality I'd always carried with me, no matter how hard I tried to keep it in check.

"Wow. I can't believe the Willa Barrett is back in town. How have you been?" Blake asked, his voice carrying that mix of curiosity and admiration I'd come to recognize—and rely on. His lingering glances in the rearview mirror felt like a spotlight, and I leaned into it, feeling exposed but also somehow powerful.

"Good," I replied, letting my eyes lock with his in the mirror. Slowly, I blinked and batted my lashes, tilting my head just enough to give him a small, shy smile. I'd already noticed the wedding ring on his finger, but it didn't matter. It wasn't about him. It was about knowing I could still draw that look—the one that said I was wanted, that I could take what I wanted if I chose to. I wouldn't, of course. But it was the wanting that mattered, the fleeting power of it. That's all it ever was with me.

Beauty has always been my currency, a passport that carried me far away from this place. I'm tall, and I've always carried my height with an ease that feels like second nature. My hair is a pale gold, the kind of blonde that shifts with the light—sometimes soft and warm, other times sharp and bright. People often comment on my eyes, pale blue and piercing, the kind that seem to hold secrets or perhaps invite questions. My face is striking, balanced in a way that draws attention without trying. My looks have opened doors, carried me places I never imagined. They took me right out of this town I always felt too good for.

"How long are you in town for?" Blake asks, his flirty smile mirroring the one I'd just given him. With it, I've already gotten everything I need from him.

"Just until Monday," I reply, turning my gaze from his eyes in the mirror, dismissing him without a second thought. My attention drifting to the window, where Jim Thorpe, Pennsylvania, slides past in a blur of familiar streets and landmarks. Each one carries a piece of me, fragments of the girl I used to be, shaped and worn by this place.

"Just the weekend," Blake confirms, ignoring the silent wall I've put up between us. "Tyler know you're in town?"

The name hits me like a jolt, pulling my eyes back to the rearview mirror before I can stop myself. Blake catches it—catches the flicker of emotion that flashes across my face before I can wrestle it back into submission. He smiles, satisfied, like he's just unearthed a secret I'd never wanted to share.

We pull up to my parents' house—or, no, just my dad's house now, I correct my mind. The thought twists something deep inside me, sharp and painful. Blake's smirk lingers in the rearview mirror as I step out of the taxi, handing him just enough cash to cover the fare. It isn't a statement—it's simply all I could afford. Still, I wish I could have stiffed him, if only to wipe that smug look off his face.

I turn toward the house, and for a moment, it feels like the past is walking right here with me, breathing down my neck. It looks exactly the same—modest and unchanging, its rectangular shape as familiar as the back of my hand. If I weren't who I am now—fractured and worn thin by the years—and if we hadn't lost so much, it could almost feel like no time had passed at all.

My old dark blue Dodge Neon, bought for me for my 16th birthday, is still sitting in the driveway like a ghost of my past self. It's a relic of a girl I barely recognize anymore. That car had carried me through so much—stolen nights, reckless freedom, and dreams that never felt too big back then. Now, it's just a reminder of everything I left behind. And everything I can never get back.

Before I can take my first step toward my dad's front door, it swings open wide, and he rushes out. He's not the man I remember, but a smaller, frailer version of himself, his once broad shoulders now stooped and his hair almost completely gray. He's wearing heavy Sorel winter boots, hastily pulled on over blue plaid pajama pants, with a deep blue dressing gown trailing behind him, brushing the edges of the recently shoveled walkway.

"Hi, Dad," I manage to say as his arms wrap around me, pulling me into him. His scent washes over me—something woody with a faint hint of citrus, a smell so familiar it hurts.

"I heard the car," he says, his voice trembling with the tears he's holding back. "I couldn't believe my eyes," he murmurs into the side of my face, his breath warm against the winter chill.

For a moment, his greeting melts me. It's nice to be loved, to be someone's child again, even if just for a second. But the warmth doesn't last long. Deep down, I know the truth. When he sees me—when he truly sees the person I've become—there's no way he could love me.

"Come in," he says as he finally pulls away from me. I feel the cold settle in the absence of his warmth, and I begin to miss how much his hugs used to cure everything when I was small. Back then, a hug was a balm for all things—a scraped knee, a bad dream, a broken heart – my parents' love fixed it all.

"Do you have a bag? Let me take that," he offers, gesturing toward the small carry-on at my side. His voice is gentle, the way it always was when he wanted to help.

I shake my head. "I've got it."

I don't explain. I don't tell him that this bag holds what's left of the life I once thought would mean so much more, or that handing it over feels like admitting just how far I've fallen. Instead, I clutch it tighter, as if the leather handle is the only thing grounding me, and step inside. Crossing the threshold feels like stepping into a memory—familiar yet distant, warm yet weighted with everything I've lost and miss so much.

Dad pulls off his boots in the hall, tucking them neatly onto the shoe tree. Mom always hated it when we left our shoes out, so I follow suit without a second thought, falling back into old habits.

The air smells the same, like time hasn't moved inside these walls. The life we lived here still lingers, woven into every corner. The foyer is painted that beautiful sage green Mom had chosen herself—a colour she'd been so proud of after painting it with her own two hands. Near the orange-tinted oak doors of the closet where all our winter coats still hung, a cross-stitch of a goose wearing a bonnet and apron hangs on the wall, a relic of her whimsical touch.

As I followed Dad further inside, it was like stepping backwards in time. The same orange-stained oak runs through every room, its glossy finish now dulled with age. The crafts Mom and I had made together, displayed proudly in years past, still hung on the walls. Now, they are coated in a fine layer of dust, but they might as well have been glowing for how vividly the memories played in my head—Mom laughing as we worked, my younger self beaming at her praise.

We walked through the living room, where we used to watch movies every Friday as a family. It was the only night we were allowed to eat in front of the television, and the memory tugged at something tender inside me. Everything was as I remembered, but the weight of time pressed down on the familiarity.

Finally, we reached the kitchen—the heart of every family dinner, every celebration. I could almost see Mom again, proudly presenting me and Dad with a chocolate cake made from scratch, the way she always did for special occasions. The room felt alive with memories: celebratory dinners for every milestone—my first day of kindergarten, my first lost tooth, passing my driving test on the first try, my high school graduation. And then, the last one. The night I left.

This house, this room, this family—everything had revolved around me. My parents had made me the centre of it all. And I left.

"Would you like some tea?" Dad asked, his voice pulling me out of my reverie.

I turn away from the oak table, where the ghosts of time seem to be playing dress-up as my family, frozen in moments that feel both distant and painfully close. My gaze shifts to Dad, and I wonder what he's thinking. He looks almost grateful to have me here, like he's holding onto the relief of my presence without questioning it too deeply. But I know he doesn't understand why I've come. Truthfully, neither do I.

"Tea would be lovely, Dad," I said, offering the tiniest of smiles.

We sit at the table, sipping the warm chamomile—Mom's favourite. She used to drink a cup every night before bed, a small comfort at the end of each day. Now, in her absence, Dad has adopted the same ritual. The steam rises between us, but the silence lingers longer than the warmth of the tea.

It's me who finally speaks, breaking the stillness.

"I was hoping I could stay," I say, my voice soft, my gaze fixed on the teacup in my hands, unwilling to meet Dad's eyes across the table.

"I was hoping," Dad replies instantly, his tone unguarded, and it scares me. I know too well what my leaving did to Mom and Dad—how the dreams I chased left them in the wreckage. And they aren't the only ones who paid the price.

"How long will you stay?" he asks, his voice tinged with something fragile.

"Until Monday?" I answer, the question in my tone betraying my uncertainty.

"Oh." The disappointment in Dad's voice is immediate, and it slices through me. "So, not for Christmas then?" His voice carries a plea, one that I can't bring myself to acknowledge. I know I cannot stay here for an extra week.

"I have to get back," I mumble, barely lifting my eyes. The words feel hollow even as I say them. Of course, I don't have to get back. I don't have anything to get back to.

My life might look beautiful on Instagram, but it's nothing more than a polished lie. I am a polished lie. My perfect boyfriend, Justin? He's a co-worker at the bar where I barely scrape by. Every now and then, he humours me by letting me snap a photo of us together, but I doubt he'd be so generous if he knew I was posting them, pretending we were a couple. I think his wife would like it even less.

The ring I'd captioned "the best surprise of my life" wasn't a gift. It was an image I found on a discount website, blurred and edited just enough to make it look convincing.

The house in my photos—the one bathed in golden light, its yard perfectly manicured—isn't mine. It's a house I pass every day on my walk to work, the same walk that reminds me I can't even afford a car. Sometimes I take a picture of the car parked in the driveway, pretending it's mine, too.

I post smiling photos with captions about roles I've never even auditioned for, announcements for opportunities that don't exist. My career ended when my agent dropped me over a year ago. There's nothing on the horizon now—just the weight of my failures, the quiet hum of regret, and the steady comfort of something strong in my glass at the end of the day.

Even my cat, Tina—the only real thing I've ever posted—left me. I tell myself she found a better home, one she didn't feel the need to escape.

I don't have anything to get back to. But I can't stay here either.

"I understand," Dad says quietly as he clears our mugs, rinsing them in the sink before setting them neatly in the dish rack to dry. "I'll make up your bed for you."

I follow him up the stairs, each step creaking under our weight, as if the house itself remembers the youth, the promise and the potential that once lived here. The echoes of a girl who dreamed big enough to outgrow it all.

At the top of the stairs, the door to my old bedroom is closed. When Dad swings it open, I am tugged into the past. Everything is the same. The twin bed with its slightly sagging canopy, the pine dresser standing resolute against the pastel purple walls Mom let me choose when I was six. Even the posters of Fall Out Boy and Panic! At The Disco still cling to the walls, their corners curling with age, as though they've been waiting for me to come back.

Dad enters the room with an armful of bedding, his movements slower now, careful. He starts to make the bed.

"I'll do it, Dad," I say softly, watching the fragility in him that wasn't there before. He hesitates for a moment, then hands me the sheets and steps back, letting me take over.

"Okay," Dad says softly, his voice barely above a whisper. "I'm going to head to bed. Do you need anything?"

I glance over my shoulder at him. "I'm okay, Dad," I reply, my voice steady enough to convince him, if not myself.

He lingers in the doorway, his presence warm even in its hesitation. "I'm glad you're here," he says, and then he pads quietly down the hall, his footsteps muffled by the worn carpet.

I finish making the bed and slip under the musty quilt, the fabric faintly carrying the scent of time and disuse. The soft purple lilacs on its surface are faded now, the colours dimmed by age and countless washes. Mom and I had picked it out together, back when everything felt simple.

Lying on my back, I stare up at the canopy above me, its once-bright fabric now dulled slightly, and I can't help but feel her here. Mom is in everything—woven into the walls, the air, the memories that cling to this house. She feels so close, as though her presence is stitched into my very skin.

We were inseparable when I was growing up. She was my everything—my confidante, my protector, my friend. I told her everything, and she always made it better. When I was lonely, she filled the space. When I was scared, she stood between me and the world.
But that closeness eroded as I grew. I became something else—something wild, rebellious, desperate to fight against the boundaries that felt like prison walls. I wanted freedom, even if I didn't know what to do with it.

I remember the night I left. I remember her face, the way her words cut me deeper than I could admit. "You're unrecognizable," she said, her voice trembling with sadness, not anger. Her final words to me before I walked out the door. And I vowed, in that moment, that if she didn't recognize me now, she wouldn't recognize me when I was a star, when the world finally saw what I was capable of.

And then I left.

His name was Axel. He smoked hand-rolled cigarettes and always smelled faintly of tobacco and rebellion. He had a car, a shaved head, and both nostrils pierced—a look that made him seem dangerous and exciting in a way Tyler never could. He was 22. Compared to Tyler, Axel wasn't just older; he was a man. At least, that's the way I saw it at 17.

He'd been living in Allentown with his aunt, and it was his beat-up car I climbed into the night I decided to leave everything behind. I was chasing the big, open world—the one where dreams were supposed to come true. We headed west on I-70 with hearts full of defiance and possibility. But we didn't make it far. By the time we reached Columbus, Ohio, Axel left me stranded at a gas station. I came out of the restroom to find his car gone, the echo of its engine fading into the distance, leaving nothing of him behind but the sting of betrayal.

I knew Mom would have come to get me if I'd called. I knew she would have driven for hours without hesitation, taken me back home, and folded me into the comfort I knew was always waiting there for me. But I was 17—stubborn, proud, and desperate to escape. So instead, I bought a Greyhound ticket with the crumpled cash I had left and took the bus the rest of the way to Los Angeles, clinging to a dream I barely understood.

I never saw Axel again. And piece by piece, the version of myself I thought I was began to peel away.

Now, back in my childhood bed, staring up at fabric almost as faded as me, it wasn't Axel I was thinking of. It was Tyler. It was the girl I'd been in his eyes—the one he saw when he looked at me sideways, one hand on the wheel of his truck as we cruised the backroads outside Jim Thorpe. The windows were down, my hair tangling in wild tendrils around my face, and his blue eyes meeting mine in the rearview mirror, steady and unflinching. I felt exposed under his gaze, vulnerable in a way that made my heart race, but I revelled in it.

His laugh would drift over the sound of gravel crunching beneath the tires, and we'd sing along to the radio—our song wasn't even a song, just the music of those nights: the hum of the engine, the rustling of trees, and the unspoken promises we didn't yet know we couldn't keep.

It was those moments—the ones etched into the backroads and the breeze through my hair, the hum of his truck and the way Tyler looked at me like I was everything—that brought me back to Jim Thorpe. Those nights with him were the last time I felt whole, the last time I felt alive, when I was brand new. Before I did everything wrong. Before I made every choice that led me further from the girl I'd been when his blue eyes met mine. Coming back here felt like chasing something I'd lost, a version of myself I didn't know if I could ever find again. But Tyler was here, somewhere, and he was the only part of me that had ever felt right.

The following morning, I slept until 11. A gentle knock at the door and the smell of bacon pulled me from sleep. The door creaked open, and Dad poked his head in. "I made breakfast," he said. "I wasn't sure what time you'd get up."

Only my eyes peeked out from under my old quilt. The chill of the Pennsylvania air had seeped into the house overnight, but instead of discomfort, it brought a strange kind of solace. The cold, my bed, this house, my dad—all of it felt like a comfort I hadn't known I missed. For a moment, I felt close to myself, to the girl I used to be, as if the woman I had become had fallen away almost entirely.

"I'll be down in just a minute," I replied, my voice muffled by the quilt.

Dad lingered in the doorway; his presence warm but hesitant. It was so like us—lingering silences, words left unsaid. Is this why I had come here? To remind myself, and to remind him, of all the unspoken things that had cut deep into our relationship?

"Okay," he finally said before slipping back into the hall and closing the door softly behind him. I listened to his footsteps retreat down the stairs, each creak of the old wood echoing in the quiet.

I sighed and sat up, the weight of the quilt slipping off me. I wished I were stronger, wished I could find the words to fill the spaces we'd left barren between us. Instead, I let the silence linger, pulling on a heavy wool sweater and a pair of jeans before heading downstairs.

In the kitchen, the smell of bacon mingled with brewing coffee. Dad had set the table with a kind of care that caught me off guard: plates, napkins, and even a little jar of strawberry jam that had probably been sitting in the fridge since summer.

"Help yourself," he said, gesturing to the pan of scrambled eggs and the plate of bacon on the counter. "I wasn't sure how hungry you'd be.

"This looks great, Dad," I said, and I meant it. There was something about the caring gesture—the simplicity of it—that I hadn't experienced in years, even from myself.

I opened the cupboard to grab a plate, my hand instinctively reaching for its usual spot—exactly where it had always been. Nothing in this kitchen had moved in 12 years. The same neatly stacked dishes, the same slightly worn handles, the same sense of order that made it feel like I had never left, even though I had.

I turned back to Dad, offering a small, hesitant smile as I scooped eggs onto my plate, adding two pieces of toast and a couple of slices of bacon. He watched me over the rim of his coffee mug but said nothing.

After sitting down across from him, I broke the bacon into halves, placing it on the toast and spreading a thin layer of strawberry jam on top. It was the way I'd eaten bacon since I was a little girl.

"Your very own recipe," Dad commented with a nod toward my plate.

"It's still delicious," I replied, and we both laughed. The sound filled the room, warm and fleeting, dissolving into another long silence. The only sounds left were the crunch of bacon, the soft clink of forks against plates, and the faint swallows of coffee.

When we finished, Dad began clearing the table.

"Let me," I said, standing. There was a moment of back-and-forth protest before the doorbell rang, and dad relented, agreeing to let me clean up as he went to answer the door.

As I began filling the sink with warm water, Dad returned to the kitchen. "It's actually for you," he reported. "Let me take over." He sidled up beside me, slipping his hands into yellow rubber gloves to begin the dishes.

Curiosity tugged me toward the front door, and as I reached the foyer, my breath caught in my throat. Tyler stood there, framed in the doorway like something out of a dream I hadn't let myself have in years. My heart fluttered, my pulse quickening as I took him in.

He was tall, taller than I remembered, his broad shoulders filling the space like he'd grown into himself in ways I hadn't imagined. His thick, dark chestnut hair still had that natural tousle, the kind that always looked effortlessly perfect, with soft wisps brushing against his forehead. And those eyes—God, those eyes—a blue so piercing and vibrant they seemed to see straight through me. When he smiled, it wasn't just a smile; it was warmth, familiarity, and everything I wanted to wrap myself up in.

"Hi, Willa," he said, his voice steady and rich, each word wrapping around me like a song I hadn't heard in years. For a moment, the world tilted slightly beneath me. I melted, every part of me aching for the simplicity of what we once were—uncomplicated, innocent, and full of promise.

"Blake texted, said you were in town," Tyler continued, a hint of shyness tugging at the corners of his charming smile. "I guess I wanted to see it for myself."

I felt my lips curve into a bashful, instinctive smile. "Well, here I am," I said softly, the words feeling heavier than I intended, as if they carried all the years between us.

"Yes, here you are," he grinned. "How long are you here for?"

"Until Monday," I replied, my heart still fluttering and threatening to choke me. I couldn't think of anything else to say.

"Oh, okay," Tyler replied. "Just the weekend then. I thought, if you had time, we could go for a coffee, or a drink, or something? Just catch up, you know."

"I—" I started to reply but stopped, unable to think of what to say next. What was I hoping here? What could I say? I'll meet you for a drink, we'll rekindle everything we had from twelve years ago, and live happily ever after? I will just magically be brand new, and not a girl who let everything slip through her fingers?

We stood there, our eyes locked, seeing only each other as if the world around us had faded. His hands were in his pockets, his posture hesitant. He owed me nothing, and yet, here he was.

"I..." I started again, but the words tangled in my throat, stuck beneath the weight of everything unsaid. Still, I couldn't finish. I couldn't think clearly. I couldn't get anything out.

"I understand," he said quietly, his smile slipping from his face. And as it faded, my heart sank back to its resting place—withered and buried deep within my chest.

In that moment, I pictured that same smile faltering as we sat together in his truck, the cab thick with silence and heartbreak, our entire future slipping away as I told him I was leaving.

We had been planning for a life together. I was supposed to join Tyler at Lehigh University in Bethlehem, just 25 miles outside of Jim Thorpe. We'd spent so many weekends poring over apartment listings, dreaming about what it would be like to share a space, to share a life. We imagined studying together at our tiny kitchen table, making late-night coffee runs, building something that was entirely ours.

We'd even talked about our bedroom—choosing a bedspread and little knickknacks from a local shop in Jim Thorpe, imagining how magical it would feel to collapse into each other's arms at the end of each long day. We had plans, dreams that felt as real as the stars we used to stare at from the bed of his truck. But as I told him I was leaving, all of it—every dream, every promise—disappeared along with his smile.

I met Axel at a party in Allentown. Megan, my best friend back then, had been dating an older guy named Braydon for a few months. Braydon was the kind of boy our parents warned us about—reckless, brash, and thrilling in a way that felt like rebellion. It was a secret we kept from Megan's parents and her older sister, Jess. That secrecy made it feel exciting, forbidden, dangerous and sexy.

I had been the first of my friends to get a car, so when Braydon invited Megan to a party in the city, I became her automatic plus-one. The drive felt exhilarating, like we were stepping into a life that was bigger, bolder, more real than the one we'd known.

When we arrived, Braydon was already drunk. He grabbed Megan's hand and they disappeared into the crowd, leaving me alone in a sea of strangers. That's when I saw Axel.
He was leaning against a wall, a cigarette dangling from his lips, his head tilted just enough to send his thick, dark hair falling into his eyes. He was older—twenty-two, I would learn later—with broad shoulders and a casual confidence that seemed magnetic. His piercing blue eyes caught mine across the room, and in that instant, I felt like I'd been seen for the first time.

"Hey," he said as I drifted closer, his voice low and smooth. "You don't look like you belong here."

"Neither do you," I shot back, trying to sound bold. He laughed, a deep, warm sound that made my stomach flip.

The night blurred after that. Axel stayed by my side, his attention unrelenting, his words spinning stories of places I'd never been and lives I'd never imagined. He was everything Tyler wasn't—worldly, confident, and just dangerous enough to feel thrilling.

By the end of the night, we were outside. The air was cold, but Axel's presence felt warm, magnetic. We sat in his car, his hand brushing against mine, and I didn't pull away. The way he looked at me made me feel older, more alive, and I let myself believe I was. When I left the party that night, I wasn't the same girl who had arrived.

For the next three months, Axel became my secret. I told myself it was harmless—that it didn't mean anything, that it was just an escape. But every stolen moment I spent with him made Tyler feel smaller, more boyish. Axel made me feel grown-up, like I was stepping into a bigger, more exciting world, and I started to resent the simplicity of what Tyler and I had built. Our late-night phone calls, once so comforting, began to feel childish. Sneaking out to sit on the old tire swing in my front yard, talking about dreams that suddenly seemed so small, felt like something teenagers would do—something I was too old for now. And the more we talked, the less I wanted to hear the melody of the song that had once been ours. What had once felt timeless now felt overplayed, dated, and far too small for the person I thought I was becoming.

With Axel, it was more. It was hunger—raw and consuming. We would lose ourselves in each other, night after night, our bodies tangled in ways that felt both electric and inevitable. He worshipped me with a devotion that left me breathless, his touch igniting something primal and deeply alive within me. Every time, it felt like magic, like stepping into a world where nothing else existed but us.

It was Axel who first told me I was too beautiful for Jim Thorpe. "You've got a Hollywood face," he said one afternoon, a cigarette dangling from his lips and his voice dripping with certainty and longing. "You're wasting your time here. You should be in LA, making movies. You've got that look—young, sexy, unforgettable."

"You really think so?" I'd asked, the words trembling with hope.

"I know so," he said, leaning closer. "I could be your agent, Willa. I know people. I could help you."

I believed him. I wanted to believe him. He made me feel like the world was mine for the taking, like all I had to do was reach out and grab it. It was intoxicating.

That night in Tyler's truck was the night I let it all unravel. The stars above us were bright, scattered across the sky like shards of glass, sharp and severe. Tyler sat beside me, his hands gripping the steering wheel, his knuckles white.

"I need to tell you something," I said, my voice trembling.

He turned to me, his blue eyes searching mine. "What is it?"

"I met someone," I admitted, the words heavy in the air between us. "It's not fair to you, Tyler. I can't keep pretending."

His face crumpled, his jaw tightening as he looked away. The silence that followed was unbearable, stretching out like an open wound.

"I thought we had a plan," he finally said, his voice breaking. "We were supposed to do this together. You and me."

"I know," I whispered, tears stinging my eyes. "But things changed. I changed."

He nodded slowly, his eyes fixed on the horizon. "I hope you find what you're looking for, Willa," he said, his voice barely audible.

Now, as Tyler turned from me in my dad's house, closing the door behind him, it felt like another ending. Just like that night in the truck, I watched him leave, and I was left with the hollow ache of everything I'd lost.

"Willa," my dad's voice called from the kitchen, low and steady, but carrying an edge that froze me in place.

I swiped at my cheeks, surprised to find them damp with tears I hadn't realized were falling. I sniffed, trying to collect myself, and turned to head back to the kitchen, forcing confidence into my stride.

The moment I stepped through the doorway, my confidence evaporated. Dad wasn't at the sink where I'd left him, halfway through the dishes. He was seated at the kitchen table, the same spot where we'd been eating breakfast seemingly just moments ago. Before him, standing like a silent witness, was the empty vodka bottle I had pilfered from the freezer.

My stomach dropped.

I'd taken it after sneaking downstairs. I'd sat right there at that very table, staring out into the backyard. The wooden playhouse Dad had built for me all those years ago still stood, though it leaned heavily to one side now, dilapidated and forgotten. But to me, it still rang with echoes of my childhood—the girlish voice that had been mine once, summoning princesses and dinosaurs from the depths of my imagination.

The ghosts of the past had crowded around me as I sat there, their joyous haunting wrapping me in a suffocating embrace. One slug of vodka after another burned my throat, and the tears poured freely until I felt none of it. Until the ghosts finally retreated, lulled to sleep by the numbing haze I'd wrapped myself in.

I thought I'd hidden the evidence, tucking the bottle deep into the garbage bin and burying it under empty cans and yesterday's coffee grounds. But he'd found it.

"We need to talk," Dad said, his voice cutting through the thick silence. His hands were steepled in front of his face, his eyes fixed on the table as if looking at me would break something in him.

My legs felt unsteady as I pulled out the chair I had been sitting in earlier. The tears came again, hot and unstoppable, and I sank into the seat with the weight of everything I'd been hiding pressing down on me.

The silence stretched, heavy and unbearable, until he finally spoke.

"You've been running, Willa," he said quietly. "Running from everything. From me. From yourself. And now, it's catching up with you."

I bit my lip, trying to hold it together, but the floodgates had already opened. The words I'd buried deep within me, the truths I'd tried so hard to silence, began clawing their way to the surface. I had nowhere left to hide.

"I'm not running," I snapped, the words spilling out before I could stop them. "I came back, didn't I? What more do you want from me?"

Dad's hands clenched into fists on the table, his calm slipping. "You came back, but you're still running, Willa. You've been running since the day you left. You think I don't see it? The way you've been hiding? The drinking? The lies? I see it all, Willa."

I shook my head, my voice rising. "You don't know anything about my life. You don't know what I've been through."

"You're right, I don't," he shot back, his voice sharp enough to cut. "Because you never let me in. You shut me out the second things got hard. You think you're the only one who lost something? You think I didn't feel it when you left? When you didn't even show up for your mother's funeral?" His voice cracked on the last word, and the weight of it hit me like a punch.

"That's not fair," I whispered, but the words felt hollow even to me. Tears burned my eyes, but I blinked them back, unwilling to let him see me break.

"Fair?" he echoed, his voice bitter and so unlike the voice of my father. "You want to talk about fair? What's fair is the way you've been lying to yourself, pretending like you've got it all together when I can see you falling apart. You're drinking yourself numb, Willa. You're killing yourself one bottle at a time, and you don't even care enough to stop."

"Stop it," I snapped, my voice shaking. "You don't understand. You don't know what it's like to feel this... empty."

"Then tell me!" he shouted, his hands slamming against the table. "For once, just tell me what you're feeling instead of drowning it in vodka and running away!"

I wished I could tell him. I wished I could tell him about the shame that hollowed me out, about the deep ache I felt every time I thought of not coming back for Mom's funeral. I remembered his offer to pay for my flight into Allentown, his voice so hopeful. And I remembered the lie I'd told him in response—that I was doing so well, killing it on the West Coast, that I didn't need his charity. The truth was, I couldn't afford anything, not even the illusion of success I'd built for myself. I thought my lies were bulletproof, but he'd seen through every one of them. Of course he had.

I thought Mom and I would have more time. Time to fix what I had shattered. I thought we'd have years to rebuild the relationship that had once been so close. I thought I'd have time to come back as the woman I wanted to be, not the mess I'd become. But then Dad called and told me about the cancer. And then the spiral. And then the end. There would be no reconciliation for us. No patched relationship. No meeting as woman to woman, sitting across from each other, sipping coffee or drinking wine, laughing over something trivial but beautiful in the way only mothers and daughters can.

How could I tell Dad about the shame that crushed me under its weight?

I couldn't. The words stayed locked inside, trapped in the same silence that had always lived between us.

I slapped my palms flat onto the table and stood abruptly, my chair scraping against the floor. My heart pounded as I headed for the front door. My eyes landed on the keys to my old Dodge Neon, still hanging on their hook by the door as if waiting for me all these years. Nothing here had changed, even though everything about me had.

I grabbed the keys without a second thought and raced out the door, slamming it behind me. I didn't give myself time to grab a coat. I didn't give myself time to think.

The cold hit me hard, biting at my cheeks, already raw from the tears that wouldn't stop falling. I fumbled with the lock on the car, my hands trembling, and climbed inside, the familiar smell of the old upholstery washing over me like a memory, but a memory was all it was. I shoved the key into the ignition, whispering a silent prayer as I turned it. The engine sputtered to life, and I gripped the steering wheel tightly, my breath coming in shallow bursts.

I just needed to get out of there. I couldn't sit at that table any longer with Dad looking at me, really looking at me, seeing every cracked piece of me laid bare. My addictions. My fear. My failure. All of it, exposed under his gaze in a way I never wanted him to see.

The car rumbled beneath me, the only sound in the stillness of the day. I wiped at my face with the sleeve of my sweater, but the tears wouldn't stop. And so, I sat there, clutching the wheel, unsure of where I could go, but knowing I couldn't stay.

The tires skidded as I backed out of the driveway, the balding rubber struggling to grip the snow-packed pavement. My heart raced in sync with the sputtering engine, but I didn't care. I pressed harder on the gas, and the Dodge Neon lurched forward, the familiar rattle of its frame shaking the silence inside the car. It hadn't been driven it in over a decade, and every sound it made reminded me of just how long it had been.

I turned onto the main road, retracing a route that felt as etched into me as my own heartbeat. The trees lining the streets, bare and skeletal, blurred past me, and for the first time in years, I felt a flicker of something almost like freedom. I was heading to Tyler's before I even realized that was my intended destination.

The car groaned beneath me, the needle on the fuel gauge dipping dangerously close to empty, but I pressed on, gripping the steering wheel tightly as the familiar landmarks came into view. The Methodist church stood tall, its steeple piercing the winter sky. Next to it, the old school loomed, its brick walls soaked in memories of Tyler, Megan, and me. Tyler had graduated the year before Megan and I, but we all walked those halls together, leaving pieces of ourselves behind in classrooms, at lockers, in whispered secrets exchanged during lunch breaks.

The engine sputtered, and I cursed under my breath, the needle now firmly resting on "E." The Neon coasted as I turned into the small lot between the church and the school, finally rolling to a reluctant stop. I shut it off and slumped back against the seat, the silence rushing in all at once.

I sat there for a moment, staring out at the fading light. The sky was painted with streaks of gray and soft lavender, the colours deepening into dusk. It felt like the world itself was holding its breath. I cursed myself for not grabbing a jacket as I stepped out, the cold biting at my cheeks again as I locked the car behind me.

The walk to Tyler's house felt longer than I remembered. With every step, the weight of the years between us pressed harder on me. By the time I reached the familiar house, the winter sky had turned fully to dusk, the last light of day fading behind me.

I stood at the edge of the driveway, staring at what was once his parents' home. I knew from Instagram that they had retired to Florida a few years ago and that Tyler had bought the house from them. He was a carpenter now, running his own renovation company. The house was his project, his labour of love. I could see the changes—the fresh coat of paint on the shutters, the new roof, the carefully mended porch steps. But there was still a ghost of his childhood here, and of our time together.

The porch swing still hung from its rusted chains, swaying slightly in the breeze. I could see us there, young and tangled together, whispering promises that felt eternal at the time. Tyler's arm draped over my shoulder, his lips brushing mine in our first, breathless kiss. I could almost feel the warmth of him against me, the way his smile made me feel like the entire world had shrunk to just the two of us.

The memory dissolved as I stepped onto the porch. The boards creaked under my weight, and I hesitated, staring at the swing for a moment longer. The past clung to this place, but it felt distant now, like trying to hold onto smoke.

I raised my hand to the door and knocked. The sound echoed through the stillness of the deepening night, each rap of my knuckles pulling me back into the present. My breath fogged the air as I waited, the anticipation tightening in my chest.

The door creaked open, and there he was, standing in the warm glow of the light spilling out from behind him. His blue eyes widened in surprise when he saw me, his hand still on the doorknob.

"Willa?" he asked, his voice soft, confused.

Before he could say anything else, I charged through the screen door, letting it slam shut behind me. Tears blurred my vision as I wrapped my arms tightly around him, burying my face in his chest. His body stiffened at first, his arms hovering at his sides before he reluctantly returned the embrace, his hands settling awkwardly on my back.

"Willa," he said again, more firmly this time. "What's wrong?"

I didn't answer. I couldn't. Instead, I tilted my face up to him, tears streaking my cheeks, and kissed him.

At first, he didn't respond. His lips were still, unmoving against mine, and panic gripped me. I started to pull away, my heart sinking, but then his hands tightened on my waist, pulling me back to him.

The hesitation was gone. His lips pressed against mine, soft at first, as if testing the waters, but then something shifted. The kiss deepened, turned hungry, desperate. His fingers slid into my hair, tangling there, and I clung to him like he was the only thing holding me together.

We stumbled backward, our movements clumsy with urgency, until my back hit the wall. His hands roamed, pulling me closer, and I couldn't get enough of him. This wasn't just a kiss. It was an unraveling, a consuming.

Everything else—the years, the distance, the pain—dissolved in the heat between us. His lips traveled from my mouth to my jaw, then to my neck, and I shivered as his breath sent a wave of warmth through me. I tugged at his shirt, my hands desperate to feel his skin beneath my fingertips, to hold onto something real.

The living room blurred around us as we moved together, his touch igniting something inside me that had long been buried. I didn't just want him—I needed him, in a way that felt like reclaiming the pieces of myself I'd lost. The Willa I'd been the last time I was here, the last time I'd felt whole, pure, happy.

He pulled me closer, his hands firm yet reverent, as though he too was searching for something in this moment, in me. The couch met the back of my knees, and I fell into it, pulling him down with me. Our bodies tangled together, the space between us disappearing completely.

This wasn't soft or slow—it was fire and ache, a desperate attempt to stitch ourselves back together, if only for a little while. His lips trailed along my collarbone, his hands exploring every curve, and I felt myself unraveling under his touch. It was overwhelming, consuming, everything I didn't know I still needed.

I wasn't just kissing Tyler. I was kissing the past, the hope, the version of myself I had once believed in. And for the first time in years, I felt like I was finding her again.

I woke to the darkness, the room silent except for the steady rhythm of Tyler's breathing against my back. We were packed tightly on his couch, his arm draped over my waist, his body curved around mine like a shield against the cold. For a moment, I stayed there, staring into the shadows of the room, the warmth of his embrace both comforting and unbearable.

I shifted carefully, trying to untangle myself without waking him. His grip tightened instinctively, his fingers pressing lightly against my stomach. I paused, holding my breath, before trying again, inching away from him. The cool air of the room hit me as I slipped out of his grasp, and I sat up, scanning the darkened room for my clothing.

"Willa?" His voice broke through the room's silence, soft and questioning. "Are you leaving?"

I froze, turning to look at him. The moonlight crept through the curtains, casting a pale glow across his face. His eyes were open now, searching mine, and I couldn't hide the way my body tensed under his gaze.

"Willa," he said again, more certain this time.

"I..." My voice faltered. I didn't have an answer. I didn't know how to explain why I was leaving, why I had come here in the first place, or how even in the heat of our passion, I had felt nothing but empty. “I don’t know.”

I reached for my clothes, pulling them on in silence. Tyler stood, wrapping the blanket from the back of the couch loosely around his waist. He flicked on the light, the sudden brightness stinging my eyes.

“Let’s sit,” he said, nodding toward the kitchen. It wasn’t a suggestion. He gestured for me to follow, and I did, my feet moving without thinking, like a reflex.

We sat across from each other at the kitchen table, the distance between us vast despite the intimacy we had shared. He moved with efficiency, opening a cabinet and pulling out a tin of cocoa powder. I watched as he heated milk on the stove, the simple, familiar act pulling me back to nights when we were teenagers, sitting at this same table, sipping hot chocolate after a long walk in the cold.

He set the mug in front of me, his own hands wrapped around a second one as he sat across from me. The steam curled upward, but I couldn’t bring myself to take a sip. My hands stayed in my lap, trembling slightly.

“I thought...” Tyler started, but then stopped. He shook his head, his brows furrowing as he studied me. “I don’t understand, Willa. You seem—on Instagram, you seem happy. Like you’re living this incredible life out there in Los Angeles.”

I laughed bitterly, the sound sharp and hollow. “Instagram’s not real, Tyler. You should know that. It’s just a highlight reel. Smoke and mirrors.”

He frowned, his blue eyes narrowing. "Then tell me what's real."

I looked down at my hands, twisting my fingers together. The words sat heavy in my throat, but they came anyway, spilling out before I could stop them. "I drink, Tyler. I drink because it's the only thing that makes everything quiet. When I wake up, it's like this weight on my chest, and it doesn't go away. Not with work, not with people, not with anything. But when I drink, it goes. Just for a little while."

His frown deepened, but he didn't interrupt.

"I'm nothing, Tyler," I said, my voice cracking. "I have nothing. I work part-time in a bar. I have no exciting roles, no family, no friends that really know me. I didn't even have the courage to come back for my mom's funeral. Do you know what that feels like? To know you're so... so empty that even the people who love you most wouldn't recognize you anymore?"

Tyler's grip on his mug tightened, his knuckles white. "Willa..."

"I tell myself it's fine, that I'll fix it someday," I went on, the tears slipping down my cheeks now. "But it's not fine. I'm not fine. And I don't know how to be."

The silence that followed was thick and suffocating. Tyler set his mug down and leaned forward, his elbows on the table.

"Why didn't you say anything?" he asked quietly. "Why didn't you tell me?"

"Because what difference would it make?" I snapped, the bitterness in my voice cutting through the air. "You think you can fix me, Tyler? That's not how this works."

"I don't want to fix you," he said, his voice firm but steady. "I just want you to stop pretending you're okay when you're not. You don't have to carry all of this by yourself, Willa. You don't have to keep running." He paused before continuing softly, his voice full of hope. "You could stay."

His words pierced through the fog of my mind, and I couldn't stop the tears that followed. "I don't know how to stop," I whispered. "I don't think I can stay."

Tyler reached across the table, his hand covering mine. His touch was warm, and for the first time in a long time, I let myself feel it.

I thought about all the roads I had taken, the detours, the dead ends, the ones that had led me here, sitting across from Tyler in his warm kitchen while the weight of my life pressed down on my chest. I looked at him—at his blue eyes, still so full of depth and hope, of promise and love. And I thought about the road I hadn't taken, the one where I had stayed, where we had built the life we dreamed of together. It looked so good to me now, shining and golden in the light of everything I had lost. But I knew it wasn't a road I could walk down anymore, not the way I was now.

Tyler didn't deserve to be subjected to the mess of who I had become. I was a woman who drank to quiet the constant noise in her head, who numbed herself to avoid feeling anything at all. My body was worn down from years of abuse I had inflicted on it, my hands sometimes trembling before I even poured the first drink of the day. I was a woman who lied without thinking, who built walls so high no one could climb them, who hadn't even been able to come home for her own mother's funeral. I was selfish. I was broken. And I had nothing to offer him but more heartbreak.

"Tyler," I said softly, my voice breaking the heavy silence between us. He looked at me, his gaze steady, searching, and for a moment, I almost couldn't continue.

"This... tonight..." I began, shaking my head as tears welled in my eyes. "It was magical. It really was. And there's a part of me that wishes I could just... let myself melt into it, stay the rest of the weekend and maybe longer. Melt into you. Into the way you call me babe, the way it feels like nothing has changed, like I'm still seventeen and everything is simple and easy and good."

His brows furrowed, and he reached for my hand, but I pulled away, wrapping my arms tightly around myself. "But I can't," I said, my voice cracking. "I can't stay, Tyler. I don't know what I came here for, but it wasn't this. Or maybe it was, but whatever I thought I'd find here, it hasn't helped. It hasn't fixed anything. I'm still... me."

"Willa," he said softly, his voice full of something I couldn't bear to hear—pity, love, or maybe both.

"I'm going back to Los Angeles," I said, the words heavy on my tongue. "I don't know why. There's nothing there for me either, but it's where I belong right now. And you don't. You don't belong in my mess, Tyler. You've built something good here, something strong. You've fixed up this house, your life, and I can't be the thing that breaks it."

He opened his mouth to argue, but I shook my head. "Don't," I whispered. "Please don't make this harder than it already is."

Tears slipped down my cheeks as I stood, my legs trembling beneath me. Tyler stood too, watching me with a look that made my chest ache, but he didn't say anything. He just stood there, the blanket from the couch still draped around him like armour.

"I'm sorry," I said, my voice barely above a whisper. "For everything."

And then I turned and walked toward the door, each step feeling like a piece of me breaking off and scattering behind me. I didn't look back. I couldn't.

I left Tyler's house with the cold biting at my skin and a deep ache in my chest. I didn't know where I was going, but my feet carried me through the quiet streets of Jim Thorpe until I saw it—the flickering neon sign of The Rusty Nail, buzzing like a broken promise in the dark. I pushed open the heavy door, the smell of stale beer and burnt grease wrapping around me like an old, familiar coat. It wasn't a place I'd ever thought I'd end up, but tonight it felt like the only place I belonged. I slid onto a cracked vinyl stool at the bar, and within an hour, I had the room. I told stories that made even the gruff bartender grin, my laugh echoing too loud in the hazy air. I clinked glasses with strangers, buying rounds I couldn't afford, basking in the fleeting warmth of their adoration. For a moment, I felt like I was something again, like I mattered. But underneath it all, I could feel it creeping back—the cold, the emptiness. The weight of myself.

I downed my last drink after the bartender shouted out last call, the sting of cheap vodka doing nothing to dull the ache inside me. The laughter and warmth of the bar had already faded, leaving me alone with my thoughts. As I stepped out into the icy night, the parking lot was silent and empty except for a single cab idling near the curb. Blake, seemingly the only cab driver working in Jim Thorpe, leaned out the driver's side window, his smirk as familiar now as the ache in my chest. I climbed in without a word, sinking into the cracked seat as the door slammed shut behind me.

We reached my dad's street just as the first light of morning broke over the horizon. The sky was tinged with pale pinks and golds, a deceptive softness against the sharp ache in my chest and the haze of alcohol clouding my mind.

Blake glanced at me in the rearview, his smirk as familiar now as the crumpled bills I would be handing him. "So, what's the story with you, Willa Barrett?" he asked, his tone playful as he shifted the car into park. "Back in town to stir up some trouble?"

I leaned back against the seat, the smell of stale cigarettes and cheap air freshener mixing with the vodka I could still taste on my breath. "Maybe," I said, flashing him a coy smile. The kind of smile I knew how to use when I didn't want anyone to see what was really happening inside.

"You were always the pretty one," Blake continued, his eyes flicking to mine in the rearview mirror. "Back in high school, I mean. You still are."

I laughed, the sound sharp and hollow. "Flattery won't get you a better tip."

"Didn't think it would," he shot back, grinning.

The car rolled to a stop, and before I could make it to the front door, I saw him—my dad, standing there in his bathrobe, the same heavy Sorel boots on his feet from the day before. He must have been waiting, watching for me to come back.

"Willa," he called out, his voice tight, the edge unmistakable.

I staggered out of the cab, swaying slightly as I made my way toward the porch. "Morning, Dad," I said, my voice too loud, too cheerful.

He didn't return my greeting. Instead, his eyes swept over me, taking in the disheveled mess I'd become—the smeared makeup, the tangled hair, the unmistakable scent of booze clinging to me like a second skin.

"We need to talk," he said, his voice sharp enough to cut through my haze.

I rolled my eyes, brushing past him toward the door. “Not now, Dad. I need to sleep.”

But he stepped in front of me, blocking my path. In his hands was my carry-on bag, the one I’d brought with me from Los Angeles. “No,” he said firmly. “You’re not staying here.”

The words hit me like a slap, sobering me just enough to feel the sting. “What are you talking about?” I asked, my voice rising. “This is my home.”

“No, Willa,” he said, his voice heavy with something that sounded like heartbreak. “Not like this. I can’t watch you destroy yourself. You can’t stay here.”

The silence that followed was deafening, broken only by the sound of Blake clearing his throat behind me, the cab still idling at the curb. I turned, my face hot with anger and shame. “Fine,” I said, grabbing my bag from my dad’s hands. “I’ll go.”

Blake was already leaning across the passenger seat to push the passenger door open for me. “Hop in, Barrett,” he said, his grin unwavering.

I climbed back into the cab, slamming the door behind me. The car lurched forward, and Blake glanced at me out of the corner of his eye. “Trouble with your dad?”

“You could say that,” I muttered, staring out the window as the familiar streets of Jim Thorpe blurred past.

We drove in silence for a while before he pulled the car off the road, the tires crunching over the snow. "Where are we going?" I asked, my voice flat.

"Nowhere yet," he said, turning to look at me with a sly smile. "Figured we could just take a little detour."

The next moments blurred together—his hand on my knee, the way his breath felt hot against my skin, the way I let him pull me across the console, his lips crashing against mine. It wasn't passion. It wasn't love. It was a transaction, a way to feel something, anything, even if it was disgust that wiped away the lingering ghost of Tyler on my skin.

When it was over, we sat in silence, the car windows fogged, the air thick with so much that I didn't want to feel. I pulled my sweater back over my head, my hands trembling as I adjusted myself in the seat.

"Drive me to the bus station," I said finally, my voice cold and distant.

Blake laughed, a sharp, ugly sound. "You're something else, Barrett," he said, starting the car. "You come back here like you're better than all of us, but you're just a used-up—"

"Stop the car," I snapped, cutting him off.

We pulled up outside the bus station, the cab coming to a jerking stop. I grabbed my bag and stepped out, my hands trembling as I fumbled with the door. "Slut!" Blake shouted after me, the venom in his voice sharp and cutting. The word hung in the air, heavy and unforgiving, sinking into me like a stone. I slammed the door shut, but it didn't matter. His voice echoed in my mind as I walked away, the sting of it clinging to me, settling into the cracks I'd tried so hard to drink away.

The bus station was almost empty when I arrived, the fluorescent lights overhead buzzing faintly in the silence. Blake hadn't said another word after his parting shot, but his voice still echoed in my head. The word slut clung to me, heavy and suffocating, settling into the spaces I'd been too afraid to confront. I clutched my bag tightly as I stepped inside, trying to shake off the weight of him, of everything.

The woman at the ticket counter barely looked up as I approached, her fingernails clicking against the keyboard. "Where to?" she asked, her voice flat and disinterested.

"Allentown," I said, my throat dry. The word came out scratchy, like it was scraping against something raw inside me.

She quoted the price, and I handed over most of what little cash I had left, my fingers trembling as I slid the bills across the counter. The ticket she handed me felt impossibly small in my hand, the paper thin and fragile, just like me.

I found a seat near the window, tucking my bag under my feet as I waited for the bus. Outside, the snow was starting to fall again, coating the streets in a fresh layer of white. It should have felt peaceful, but all I could think about was the mess I was leaving behind, and then the mess I was headed towards.

The bus ride to Allentown was long and quiet. I stared out the window, the trees and houses blurring together as we drove. My reflection in the glass looked foreign to me, like someone I used to know but couldn't quite remember. I tried to close my eyes, to sleep, but every time I did, I saw Tyler's face—the way he had looked at me, the way his voice had sounded when he said my name.

By the time we pulled into the station, my stomach was churning, and my hands were clammy. I found the airline kiosk tucked near the far end of the terminal and approached the desk, the fluorescent lights making everything feel too bright, too sharp.

The clerk glanced at my crumpled itinerary, her fingers flying over the keyboard. "You can exchange this for a flight this afternoon," she said, her tone businesslike. "But there's a change fee."

I nodded, not even asking how much. My credit card was already in my hand, and I slid it across the counter without a second thought. She handed me a new boarding pass, and I clutched it like it was the only thing tethering me to the ground. It was the only thing that could get me out of here.

The airport bar wasn't hard to find—it never was. I slipped onto a stool, the worn leather creaking beneath me, and ordered a double vodka tonic. The bartender didn't ask any questions, just slid the glass toward me with a faint nod. I took a long sip, the burn spreading through my chest like a temporary salve.

One drink turned into two, then three. The buzz dulled the edges of everything, numbing the noise in my head just enough for me to breathe. But when my flight was called, I stumbled as I slid off the stool, gripping the bar for balance.

The gate attendant eyed me warily as I handed her my boarding pass, her expression tight with concern. "Are you okay to fly, ma'am?" she asked, her voice low.

I nodded, forcing a smile I didn't feel. "I'm fine," I mumbled, steadying myself against the counter.

She hesitated, but eventually scanned my pass, waving me through. I boarded the plane and collapsed into my seat, my body heavy with exhaustion and vodka. The hum of the engines lulled me into a restless sleep, my dreams a fragmented mess of snow-covered streets and blue eyes that wouldn't leave me alone.

By the time we landed in Los Angeles, the sunlight streaming through the window felt like an assault. My head throbbed, and my mouth was dry, my body protesting every movement as I stumbled off the plane. I made my way through the terminal in a haze, stopping at a convenience store near the exit.

The bottle of vodka was cheap, the label peeling at the edges, but it was all I could afford. I twisted the cap off as soon as I stepped outside, taking a long swig that burned all the way down. The warmth spread through me, dulling the ache in my chest and the shame clawing at my throat.

I couldn't afford a cab, so I walked, the streets of Los Angeles blurring around me as I drank. By the time I reached my apartment, the bottle was nearly empty, and my legs felt like lead. I climbed the stairs slowly, each step heavier than the last, until I finally reached my door.

Inside, the air was stale and cold, as lifeless as I felt. I sank onto the couch, letting the bottle slip from my fingers. It rolled across the floor with a dull thud, coming to rest under the coffee table. I stared up at the ceiling, my chest rising and falling in shallow breaths, the cracked paint swirling in patterns I couldn't quite grasp.

This wasn't what I wanted.

I had gone back to Jim Thorpe because it had felt like home—at least, the memory of it had. But when I was there, I felt like an intruder, a ghost wandering through someone else's life. I didn't belong. Not in the streets that had felt so familiar, not in Tyler's arms, not even in the warmth of my dad's kitchen. And so I ran, back to Los Angeles, because it had to be better. Because I thought maybe this was home.

But now, lying here on this couch, I knew I was wrong. The silence pressed down on me, thick and suffocating, and the world tilted and spun around me. I wanted to go home—but I was home. And yet, I wasn't. I wanted to go home, but I had no home.

The realization hit me like a tidal wave, and I sat up too quickly, the room spinning in a kaleidoscope of light and shadow. My stomach lurched violently, and I stumbled to my feet, gripping the edge of the couch for balance. I needed to get to the bathroom.

Each step felt like wading through water, my legs heavy and unsteady. The fluorescent light over the sink buzzed loudly as I flicked the bathroom light on, the sound cutting through the haze in my mind. I staggered toward the toilet, but before I could reach it, my socked foot slipped.

My legs went out from under me, and my body twisted as I fell, my head slamming against the edge of the sink with a force that echoed through my skull. Pain exploded behind my eyes, sharp and blinding, and then everything went black.

When I woke, the world was blurry and wrong. My head throbbed with an intensity that made me nauseous, and the metallic taste of blood filled my mouth. I blinked, trying to clear my vision, but the scene around me refused to sharpen.

There was blood everywhere—on the floor, on my hands, smeared across my face. The acrid stench of vomit clung to the air, mixing with the sharp tang of copper. I tried to move, to push myself upright, but my arms buckled beneath me, and I collapsed back onto the cold, sticky tiles.

I didn't know how long I lay there, my body trembling, my breath coming in ragged gasps. The pain in my head was a relentless pounding, each throb sending waves of dizziness through me. I had to move. I had to do something.

I clawed my way toward the door, dragging myself inch by inch across the floor. The effort was excruciating, every movement sending fresh pain radiating through my skull. By the time I reached the living room, I was shaking so badly I could barely hold onto the couch.

I fumbled for my phone, my bloodied fingers slipping on the screen as I dialed. The voice on the other end sounded distant and mechanical, as though it was coming from underwater.

"911, what's your emergency?"

"I fell," I slurred, my words thick and disjointed. "I hit my head. There's blood..." My voice cracked.

"Ma'am, can you tell me your name?"

"Willa," I whispered, barely able to get the word out. "Willa Barrett."

"Is there anyone we can call?" Someone asked me, maybe the 911 operator, of maybe someone else. I didn't know.

My mind swirled with faces, but only one came to the surface. "My dad," I mumbled. "Call my dad."

Time lost meaning. I drifted in and out of consciousness, the world around me a fragmented blur of flashing lights, the hum of machines, and voices I couldn't place. I floated between dreams and reality, caught in the pull of something I couldn't name.
When I finally opened my eyes, the light was dim, a soft glow casting long shadows on the walls. My head felt heavy, the ache dull but persistent, and my body was weak, as though I'd been drained of everything.

And then I saw him.

My dad was sitting beside me, his face pale and drawn, his hands wrapped tightly around mine. His eyes, rimmed red and glassy, met mine as a tear slipped down his cheek.

"Willa," he said, his voice breaking as he leaned closer.

Tears welled in my eyes, and I felt the dam inside me crack, the weight of everything pressing down at once. For the first time in years, I let myself feel the crushing reality of who I'd become—and the fragile thread of hope that someone still cared.

"I'm here," he whispered, his grip tightening as though he was afraid I might slip away again. "I'm not going anywhere."

When I opened my eyes again, the world was a blur of white and shadow. The ceiling tiles above me swam in and out of focus, the fluorescent lights buzzing softly overhead. My head throbbed with a dull, persistent ache, and my body felt impossibly heavy, like I was sinking into the mattress beneath me.

And then I felt it—his hand, warm and steady, wrapped around mine.

“Willa,” my dad’s voice broke through the fog, low and thick with emotion. I turned my head slowly, my neck stiff and protesting, and saw him sitting beside me, his face pale and drawn, his eyes still red-rimmed.

“Dad,” I croaked, my voice barely above a whisper.

He exhaled sharply, like he’d been holding his breath for hours, and squeezed my hand. “You scared me,” he said, his voice trembling. “I thought... I thought I was going to lose you.”

Tears welled in my eyes, but I couldn’t let them fall. I couldn’t bear to. “I’m sorry,” I whispered, the words catching in my throat.

He shook his head, his grip on my hand tightening. “Don’t,” he said. “Don’t say you’re sorry. Just tell me... tell me this isn’t going to happen again.”

I looked away, my chest tightening. I wanted to promise him, to tell him I’d never put him through this again. But the words wouldn’t come. I didn’t trust myself enough to say them.

The hospital released me the next day with a list of instructions and a warning about concussions. They handed me papers like they were handing me a solution, but no neatly printed checklist could address the real damage. No sheet of medical advice could undo the years I'd spent drinking myself into oblivion, trying to escape a pain I couldn't even name.

When we arrived at my apartment, I hesitated in the doorway. The space felt alien. Too quiet. Too clean. My dad had been here while I was in the hospital. The empty shelves and bare countertops were a far cry from the chaos I'd left behind. The bathroom door was ajar, and I knew without looking that he'd scrubbed away every trace of the blood and vomit. Every stain that had marked my spiral was gone, as though he thought he could erase my failures with a sponge and bleach.

My bag was sitting on the couch, neatly packed, its zipper pulled tight like it held all the pieces of my broken life. My dad stood beside it, his expression unreadable, his silence weighing heavier than any words.

"I want to take you somewhere," he said finally, his voice firm.

I froze, my heart sinking. I knew what he meant.

"Dad..." My voice cracked, and I shook my head, backing away. "No. I'm not... I'm not ready."

"You don't have to be ready," he said, stepping closer. "You just have to try."

"I can't," I said, my voice rising, panic creeping into the edges of my words. "You don't get it, okay? I'm not worth saving. I'm not... I don't deserve this."

"Willa," he said, his tone sharper now, cutting through the fog in my mind.

"Stop it. Don't say that."

"It's true!" I yelled, the words bursting out of me. "Look at me! Look at what I've done. To myself. To Mom. To you. I'm a mess, Dad. A disaster. I can't fix this."

He stared at me, his jaw tightening, his eyes shining with tears and something I couldn't bear to see. "You think I don't know that you're hurting?" he said, his voice shaking. "You think I don't see the way you hate yourself? You think I don't blame myself for not stopping this before it got this bad?"

I blinked, stunned into silence.

"I love you, Willa," he continued, his voice breaking. "Even when you don't love yourself. Even when you make it impossible. And I will not stand here and watch you throw yourself away. You are my daughter! You are all I have left."

Tears streamed down my face, and I shook my head, trying to push him away, but his words had already hit their mark. "I don't know how to fix this," I whispered, the fight draining out of me.

"You don't have to know," he said softly, stepping closer and placing a hand on my shoulder. "That's why I'm here. Let me help you, Willa. Let me do this for you."

I looked at him, my chest heaving with sobs, the weight of his words cracking something deep inside me. For the first time, I didn't feel the walls I'd built holding me up. I didn't feel their protection. I just felt... tired.

"Please," he said again, his voice a whisper. "Just come with me. That's all I'm asking."

I nodded, barely able to get the motion out through my trembling. He squeezed my shoulder and handed me the duffel bag, his grip steady. "Let's go," he said, his voice calm but resolute.

As we stepped out into the bright light of day, I felt exposed, raw, and terrified. But there was something else there too, faint but unmistakable—a flicker of hope.

We drove in silence, the hum of the engine of dad's rental car the only sound between us. I stared out the window, watching the city blur past, my reflection in the glass a ghost of the person I used to be.

The truth was, I didn't know who I was without alcohol. I drank to quiet the noise in my head, to fill the void that had been growing inside me for years. It started out as a way to take the edge off, to make the world a little softer, a little more bearable. But somewhere along the line, it became the only way I knew how to exist.

"I don't know if I can do this," I said finally, my voice barely audible.

Dad glanced at me, his eyes steady. "You don't have to do it alone," he said.

The words hit me harder than I expected, and I turned away, biting my lip to keep the tears at bay. "I don't even know who I am anymore," I whispered.

"You're Willa," he said firmly. "You're my daughter. And I love you."

The tears came again, hot and unstoppable, and I didn't bother wiping them away. The weight of his words pressed against the walls I'd built around myself, cracking them, letting in slivers of what might have been light.

The rehab centre was a sprawling complex surrounded by manicured gardens, the kind of place that looked inviting from the outside but filled me with a bone-deep fear.

"I can't do this," I said again, shaking my head as my hands gripped the edges of the seat.

"Yes, you can," my dad said, his voice steady but thick with emotion. "And you will."

I turned to him, my face streaked with tears. "I'm sorry," I whispered.

He reached out, his hand cupping my cheek. "You don't have to be sorry," he said, his voice breaking. "Please just try."

I nodded, the lump in my throat too big to speak around.

When I stepped out of the car, my legs felt weak, my body trembling as I approached the front doors. My dad walked beside me, his hand on my shoulder letting me know he was there for me.

At the entrance, I turned to him one last time. "I'm scared," I said, my voice cracking.

"I know," he said, pulling me into a tight hug. His body shook with silent sobs, and I let myself collapse into him, letting his strength hold me up.

When he finally let go, his eyes were red and swollen, matching mine. "I'll be here when you're ready," he said softly.

I nodded, stepping through the doors. The weight of the past pressed down on me, but for the first time, I felt the faintest flicker of hope.

Holding On, Letting Go

Rehab wasn't anything like I'd imagined. I had expected it to feel cold and clinical, a place filled with fluorescent lights and judgment. But it wasn't like that. Not entirely.

The mornings started early, with group therapy at eight. At first, I hated it—sitting in a circle of strangers, talking about things I wasn't ready to say out loud. But after a week, I found myself listening. And then, little by little, I started to talk.

The afternoons were quieter, reserved for reflection, journaling, or optional activities. I spent most of my time in the garden, where rows of flowers and vegetables grew under the care of people like me—people trying to piece themselves back together. The work was simple, grounding. Pulling weeds, planting seeds, watering the soil. It gave my hands something to do, my mind a chance to rest.

Evenings were the hardest. The stillness always brought the cravings, the memories, the ache. But there was something comforting about the routine here, the way the staff always made sure there was hot tea and a warm light on in the lounge. It felt safe, even when nothing else did.

It was on one of those evenings, after group therapy, that I found the letter. A staff member handed it to me during mail call, the envelope thick and slightly crumpled. My name was scrawled across the front in familiar handwriting, and my breath caught in my throat when I saw the return address.

Tyler.

My hands trembled as I sat down in the corner of the couch, the envelope heavy in my lap. For a moment, I just stared at it, my mind racing. I wasn't sure I was ready for whatever was inside, but I couldn't ignore it either. Slowly, I tore it open, unfolding the pages inside.

Willa,

I don't even know how to start this. I've been sitting here for twenty minutes, staring at this blank page, trying to find the right words. I guess I'll just start with the truth: I miss you. I miss the girl you used to be, and I miss the woman I think you're trying to become.

When you showed up at my door, it felt like the past and the present collided all at once. Seeing you brought back everything—those nights on the porch swing, the plans we made, the way you used to look at me like I was the only person in the world. I don't know if I can explain how much those memories mean to me, even now.

But I also saw the pain in your eyes. I saw how much you were carrying, and it broke my heart. I wanted to fix it, to fix you, the way I used to patch up the broken chairs in my parents' dining room. But I know now that's not how it works. I can't fix you, Willa. And I'm sorry for that night and for thinking I could.

You're stronger than you think. I know you don't believe that right now, but I see it. I see it in the way you showed up at my door, even if you didn't know why. I see it in the way you've survived things and carried on while in pain. You've made it this far, and I think that counts for something.

I don't know what's next for you, and I don't know if I'll ever see you again.

But I want you to know that I'll always be rooting for you. You're a part of me, Willa, and you always will be. I'm not angry at you. I'm not holding onto anything except hope–that you'll find what you're looking for, that you'll find yourself again.

Take care of yourself, okay? You deserve that. You deserve good things, even if you can't see it yet.

Love,
Tyler

I folded the letter carefully, my hands trembling as I placed it back in the envelope. The tears came slowly at first, then all at once, until my shoulders shook with the weight of them. I hadn't realized how much I needed to hear those words until they were in front of me, staring back at me in Tyler's familiar handwriting.

He was right. I didn't know what was next. But I felt like maybe I could figure it out. Maybe I could be okay.

As I sat there in the quiet of the lounge, the letter clutched tightly in my hands, I let myself believe—just for a moment—that there was a road forward. And maybe, just maybe, I could take it.

Life after rehab wasn't a straight road. It was winding, full of detours, and some days, I didn't even know if I was moving forward. But for the first time in years, I was walking it sober.

When the day came to leave the centre, my dad was there, waiting for me. His face lit up when he saw me, and I felt a pang of guilt for all the times I'd made him worry. But there was something else too—gratitude. For not giving up on me when I had given up on myself.

"Where to now?" he asked as we loaded my duffel bag into the trunk.

The answer came to me slowly, as if it had been forming in the quiet corners of my mind all along. "Maine," I said.

His brows furrowed in surprise. "Maine?"

"Yeah," I said, nodding. "I need somewhere new. Somewhere quiet. I don't want to go back to LA, and I can't... I can't go back to Pennsylvania. Maine feels like a fresh start."

And so, a week later, we were standing in the doorway of a small apartment in a coastal town I'd only seen in pictures. The walls were bare, the furniture sparse, but it felt like something I could grow into. My dad stayed for a few days, helping me settle in, stocking the fridge, and giving me space to breathe. He'd brought with him my mom's guitar, the one she had taught me to play so many years before.

"You'll be okay," he said before he left, his hands resting on my shoulders. "You're stronger than you think, Willa. Remember that."

I nodded, though my throat was tight with emotion. “Thank you,” I whispered.

The job he helped me find wasn’t glamorous. I worked part-time at a local bookstore, shelving dusty novels and chatting with the occasional customer. It wasn’t much, but it was enough. Enough to keep me grounded, enough to remind me that I could start over.

In my spare time, I wrote. Not stories, but songs. I’d always loved music, the way it could capture a moment, a feeling, a truth you couldn’t put into words any other way. Holding my mom’s guitar, I felt close to her again.

The first few songs I wrote were messy, fragments of thoughts and memories scribbled in the margins of my notebooks. But then the words started to flow, and the melodies came with them.

One night, sitting at the small desk by my window, I started writing a song I hadn’t realized was in me. It wasn’t about where I was now but where I had been. About a boy I had loved when I was seventeen, and the memories that had stayed with me, frozen in time.

Tyler wasn’t a part of my life anymore. He hadn’t been for years. But his memory remained perfect, untouched by the years that had passed. He was still the boy who kissed me on his porch swing, who held my hand in his truck, who made me feel like I was everything. I didn’t want to go back to him, not really. But I wanted to hold onto what he represented—the hope, the innocence, the love that had felt so pure.

And so, I wrote a song for him – a song for us. I wrote our song.

The Sound Of Being Seventeen

The backroads knew our secrets,
The gravel hummed our tune,
The stars hung low above us,
And whispered, "You'll leave soon."

Your hand brushed mine so softly,
A dare I couldn't take,
The air was thick with silence,
A pause we couldn't break.

Our song wasn't on the radio,
It was the sound of your truck down an old dirt road,
The wind through the trees, my heart skipping beats,
The way you looked at me like I was all you'd ever need.
Our song was the sound of being seventeen.

The porch swing creaked beneath us,
Your arm around my side,
You kissed me like a promise,
Before the world could divide.

We dreamed of tiny kitchens,
A bedspread just for two,
But dreams don't last forever,
And I was made to move.

Our song wasn't on the radio,
It was the sound of your truck down an old dirt road,

The wind through the trees, my heart skipping beats,
The way you looked at me like I was all you'd ever need.
Our song was the sound of being seventeen.

I see you in the rearview,
A shadow of the past,
Your love was like a mirror,
Reflecting a pretty picture never meant to last.

Our song wasn't on the radio,
It was the sound of your truck down an old dirt road,
The wind through the trees, my heart skipping beats,
The way you looked at me like I was all you'd ever need.
Our song was the sound of being seventeen.

The backroads still remember,
The gravel hums your tune,
And though I keep on driving,
The stars still whisper, "Soon."

As I finished the last line, I sat back, the pen slipping from my fingers. The words felt heavy and light all at once, like I had put something down that I'd been carrying for far too long.

I didn't know what the future would hold, but for the first time, I felt like I could face it. The road ahead wasn't easy, but it was mine. And maybe, just maybe, I was ready to walk it.

You've Reached The End But...
The Stories Never Stop

Songs To Stories is exactly what it sounds like—short, emotionally devastating, romantically charged, and occasionally unhinged novellas inspired by the one and only Taylor Swift. Because why simply listen to a song when you can spiral into an entire fictional universe about it?

A new novella drops on the 13th and 21st of every month, so if you have commitment issues, don't worry—you don't have to wait long for your next dose of heartbreak, longing, and characters making wildly questionable life choices in the name of love.

To keep up with the latest releases, visit BrittWolfe.com—or don't, and risk missing out while the rest of us are already crying over the next one. Your call.

See you at the next emotional wreckage.

About The Author

Britt Wolfe

Britt Wolfe was born in Fort McMurray, Alberta, and now lives in Calgary, where she battles snow, writes stories, and cries over Taylor Swift lyrics like the proud elder Swiftie she is. She loves being part of a fan base that's as passionate as it is melodramatic.

She's married to a smoking hot Australian (her words, but also probably everyone else's), and together they parent two fur-babies: Sophie, the most perfect husky in the universe, and Lena, a mischievous cat who keeps them on their toes—and their furniture in shreds.

When Britt's not writing or re-listening to "All Too Well (10 Minute Version)," she's indulging her love for reading, potatoes in all forms, and the colour green. She's also a huge fan of polar bears, tigers, red pandas, otters, Nile crocodiles, and—because they're underrated—donkeys.

Her life is full of love, laughter, and just enough chaos to keep things interesting.

Manufactured by Amazon.ca
Bolton, ON